THE CLOUD AND I

AN ADVENTURE...
DISCOVERING THE LOVE WITHIN

Words and music by GARY JAMES
Illustrations by MEGANNE FORBES

LUMINARE PRESS

WWW.LUMINAREPRESS.COM

Printed in the United States of America

Illustrations by Meganne Forbes
Cover Design and Interior Layout by Claire Flint Last

Luminare Press
438 Charnelton St., Suite 101
Eugene, OR 97401
www.luminarepress.com

LCCN: 2024901561
ISBN: 979-8-88679-488-5

Dedicated to the child within each of us...

BEFORE YOU BEGIN,
Select a link below so you can
listen to the song and/or sing along

www.InnerTunesPublishing.com/the-cloud-and-i

or scan the QR code

O once I was a dancer I could leap both far and high

One day when I was jumpin' up I landed in the sky

A cloud it came a sailin' by, it caught me by surprise

I thought I was a dreamin' I could not believe my eyes!

Hey, billowy pillowin' a flyin' in the sky
Hey, billowy pillowin' the cloud and I

The cloud it did it had a face and on it was a smile
It opened up its billow mouth and talked to me for a while
"I'm going to take you to a place where love it does abound
A magic sort of kingdom now like none you've ever found!"

Hey, billowy pillowin' a flyin' in the sky
Hey, billowy pillowin' the cloud and I

I said "Away! Awith! Awhile! Godspeed to you my friend!
If this be true let not a thought impede this journey's end!"
We sailed across the rolling plains and sands of Araby
The pyramids of Egypt and the Adriatic Sea

Hey, billowy pillowin' a flyin' in the sky
Hey, billowy pillowin' the cloud and I

Into the mountains of Tibet and jungles of Siam

Across to the Americas and on to many lands

I said, said I, "Companion, dear, when are we going to land?"

He said, said he, "When I can see, you finally understand!"

Hey, billowy pillowin' a flyin' in the sky

Hey, billowy pillowin' the cloud and I

"That we could travel far and wide, through all eternity
   a searchin' for the kingdom that would make you happy and free.
When all along that magic place has been so close at hand
Inside the self, you call yourself, awaiting your command!"

Hey, billowy pillowin' a flyin' in the sky
Hey, billowy pillowin' the cloud and I

I thought, thought I, how curious that I did never see
that what I wanted most of all was right inside of me
Now to the cloud I said "I'm grateful for this lesson true
I shall, in fact, remember that I'll not forget you!"

Hey, billowy pillowin' a flyin' in the sky
Hey, billowy pillowin' the cloud and I

The cloud did bow unto the earth and gently put me down

We broke into a dance of Love a whirlin' 'round and 'round

Alas, the cloud did break away and bid me fond adieu

I winked an eye, and said, said I, "God Bless you!"

I winked an eye, and said, said I, "God Bless you!"

GARY JAMES *is a writer, composer and singer living in Santa Barbara, California. He has performed his songs in church settings, weddings, memorial services, and concerts, and is an alumni of "Personal Stories," a reader's theater series. A two-disc CD of his original heart-centered and life-affirming music is available for purchase at:* **www.InnerTunesPublishing.com.**

MEGANNE FORBES *is a visionary artist and illustrator who lives on the California coast. Watercolor is her favorite medium. You may see her work on book and CD covers, hanging in public buildings and among the collections of your friends. She hopes her paintings have a beneficial effect and touch your heart.* **www.MeganneForbes.com**

32994814R00022